TWILIGHT COMES TWICE

by RALPH FLETCHER
Illustrated by KATE KIESLER

Clarion Books
New York

Clarion Books ⁊ a Houghton Mifflin Company imprint ⁊ 215 Park Avenue South, New York, NY 10003
Text copyright © 1997 by Ralph Fletcher ⁊ Illustrations copyright © 1997 by Kate Kiesler
The illustrations for this book were executed in oil paint. ⁊ The text is set in 18/14-point Weiss bold.

Printed in the USA
Library of Congress Cataloging-in-Publication Data

Fletcher, Ralph J.
Twilight comes twice / by Ralph Fletcher ; illustrated by Kate Kiesler.
p.   cm.
Summary: Poetic prose describes dusk and dawn and some of the activities that take place at those special times.
ISBN 0-395-84826-1
[1. Twilight—Fiction.]   I. Kiesler, Kate, ill.   II. Title.   PZ7.F634Tw   1997   [Fic]—dc21
96-50888   CIP   AC

WOZ   10   9

For Carol Wilcox, who brings light to so many children.
—*R. F.*

For Dad
—*K. K.*

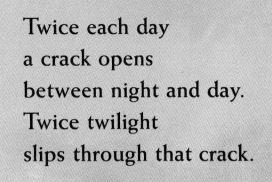

Twice each day
a crack opens
between night and day.
Twice twilight
slips through that crack.

It stays only a short time
while night and day
stand whispering secrets
before they go their
separate ways.

5

Dusk is the name
for evening twilight.
Dusk gives the signal
for night to be born.

Dusk deepens the colors
of ordinary things.
Even the common grass
takes on a luster
that makes you
stop to look.

In the summer, dusk
hisses on the sprinklers.
It flushes out
millions of mosquitoes
and armies of bats
to eat them.

Fireflies appear,
swimming through the air,
writing bright messages
in secret code.

Slowly dusk pours
the syrup of darkness
into the forest.
Crows gather in the trees
for last-minute gossip
before nightfall.

In the park, dusk
will let the kids finish,
if they hurry,
the Little League game
on the baseball diamond.

Two fishermen stand
at the edge of a lake
casting far out
into fading light.

Streetlights flicker on
in the deepening dusk.
Trains bring people home,
hungry and tired from work.

14

Dusk prepares for the great
celebration of night.
It sets the table carefully:
Venus, a few stars,
perhaps a crescent moon.

When the sky is full
and singing with stars
you know that twilight
has given way
to true night.

17

In the early morning
a pale twilight touches
the edge of the sky.
It is called dawn.
Dawn is like a seed
that will grow into daylight.

With invisible arms
dawn erases the stars
from the blackboard of night.
Soon just the moon
and a few stars
remain.

Dawn picks
bits of dark
from between
the blades of grass
in your backyard.
No job is too small.

In the forest
dawn drinks up night's
leftover darkness,
the great black pools
and deep-rooted shadows.

Walking at dawn is
a special kind of walk.
Sounds ring out more clearly.
The air is still moist
from the cool of the night
and your own skin
feels all tingly clean.

Dawn signals the crows
to start their jabbering.
What a racket they make
in the willow tree!

Down below, three robins
hop through wet grass
shopping for breakfast
worms.

Spiders rouse themselves
still stiff from the night
and go to work repairing
their dew-spangled webs.

Dawn slowly brightens
the empty baseball field,
polishing the diamond
until it shines.

At the lake
a boy sits quietly,
trying not to disturb
fish coming up to feed.

27

Streetlights flicker off.
A delivery truck leaves
a bundle of newspapers
on the sidewalk.

Outside the bakery
the smell of doughnuts
makes your stomach
rumble and growl.

As you set your table for breakfast,
dawn sets its own table,
with light that ushers in
a brand new day.